# Most Valuable Player

by
**Gilles Tibo**

illustrations by
**Bruno St-Aubin**

## Scholastic Canada Ltd.
New York  Toronto  London  Auckland  Sydney
Mexico City  New Delhi  Hong Kong  Buenos Aires

**Scholastic Canada Ltd.**
604 King Street West, Toronto, Ontario M5V 1E1, Canada

**Scholastic Inc.**
557 Broadway, New York, NY 10012, USA

**Scholastic Australia Pty Limited**
PO Box 579, Gosford, NSW 2250, Australia

**Scholastic New Zealand Limited**
Private Bag 94407, Botany, Manukau 2163, New Zealand

**Scholastic Children's Books**
Euston House, 24 Eversholt Street, London NW1 1DB, UK

www.scholastic.ca

**Library and Archives Canada Cataloguing in Publication**
Tibo, Gilles, 1951-
[Nicolas à la défense. English]
Most valuable player / Gilles Tibo ; Bruno St-Aubin, illustrator ; Petra Johannson, translator.
Translation of : Nicolas à la défense.
ISBN 978-1-4431-4598-5 (pbk.)
I. St-Aubin, Bruno, illustrator  II. Johannson, Petra, translator  III. Title.  IV. Titre: Nicolas à la défense. English
PS8589.I26N4713 2016      jC843'.54      C2015-902183-9

6  5  4  3  2  1      Printed in Malaysia  108    15  16  17  18  19

For Catherine, who is full of life.
— *G. T.*

For Antoine.
— *B. St-A.*

Nicholas was on his way to school when he met his new neighbour.

"Hi, my name's Jeremy," said the boy. "We just moved in."

"I'm Nicholas. Welcome to the neighbourhood!"

They walked to school together, talking all the way. After the first block, they had covered robots. By the end of the second block, they'd talked about biking. And on the third block, it was all about comics.

When they got to the schoolyard, Nicholas introduced his new friend.

"Hey, everyone. This is Jeremy!"

"Hi, Jeremy!"

"Welcome!"

"Hello!"

They joined the soccer game but it quickly became clear that Jeremy was not a good player. Big Dan stopped playing and rolled his eyes. Soon everyone else was following his lead, as usual.

The bell rang and everyone headed in. Jeremy followed Nicholas and chose the seat next to him. The teacher asked the class to give Jeremy a warm welcome. Everyone applauded politely but they were all looking at Dan. He was rolling his eyes even more.

That evening, Nicholas headed to the park with his friends to play soccer.

"Can I play with you guys?" Jeremy called out.

Nicholas answered, "Sure!" But nobody else even stopped.

They got to the park and started kicking the ball around. Jeremy couldn't keep up, and soon nobody would pass him the ball.

Jeremy's troubles continued when he came out to play baseball at the park. When teams were chosen, he was the last to be picked. He spent most of his time on the bench watching everyone else play, not saying a word.

It was the same with every sport. In basketball, he was able to get by the big players but he couldn't get the ball in the basket.

12

At judo, he was quick to hide between the legs of his opponents.

Every time Nicholas came to Jeremy's defence, everyone said, "What? Can't Jeremy stand up for himself?"

One morning on the way to school, Nicholas saw Jeremy sitting on his front steps. When he joined him, he could see that Jeremy's eyes were filled with tears.

Jeremy stared down at the ground. He told Nicholas what it had been like in his old town. "I didn't have many friends," he said. "And it's happening all over again."

"Well, what do you like to do best?"
Nicholas asked him.

Wiping away a tear, Jeremy answered,
"I love skating and I'd love to play hockey,
but I don't think I would be very good."

"But you're so fast!" said Nicholas. "You have all the qualities of a great scorer. All you need is some training."

"But I don't have a coach!" replied Jeremy.

"*I* know a good coach!" Nicholas smiled. "Me!"

Nicholas spent that whole school day coming up with a training plan. That night after dinner, he went over to Jeremy's with hockey sticks and balls.

The training began . . . in secret! Nicholas taught Jeremy how to control the ball, how to deke around an opponent and how to score a goal.

As the days and weeks passed, Jeremy's skills improved. He was playing like a real champion. Nicholas had to work harder and harder to block his shots.

SLAP!

As soon as it was cold enough outside, Nicholas asked his dad to make a backyard rink. Jeremy came over to practise. It turned out he was a great skater! Nicholas lent him his old hockey equipment. It was too big, but Jeremy didn't mind.

Together, they practised, practised and practised until they were worn out. Jeremy had become such a strong skater and shooter that Nicholas couldn't stop him.

One night, Nicholas's dad called Jeremy's dad, who called Nicholas's coach. The coach said that Jeremy could try out for the team at the next practice.

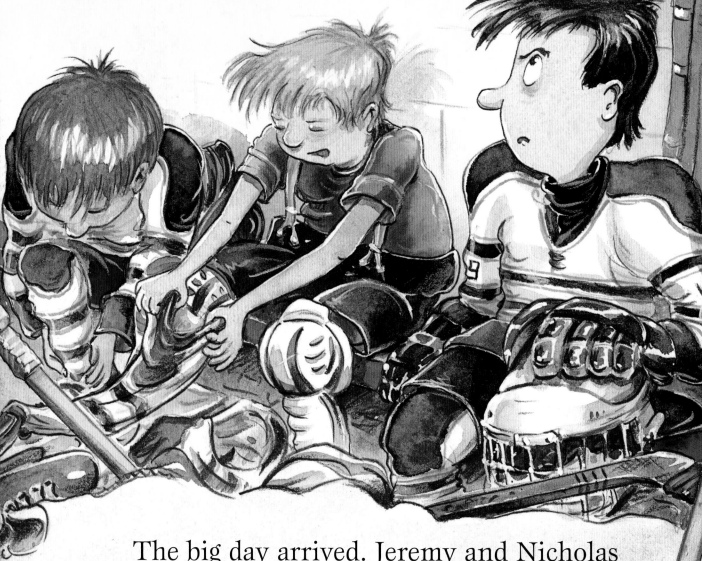

The big day arrived. Jeremy and Nicholas went to the arena together. When they walked into the dressing room, everyone rolled their eyes at Jeremy. No one said a word to him.

Jeremy and Nicholas gritted their teeth and dressed for practice. Nicholas couldn't believe how his friends were acting.

When they got on the ice, the coach split the players into two teams, and Nicholas skated to his net. Jeremy and Nicholas were on opposite sides! When Jeremy realized he was on the same team as Dan, he got so nervous that he lost his balance and fell on the ice. Everyone laughed.

Jeremy looked over at Nicholas.
Then, red as a tomato, he got up and
joined the rest of his team.

The coach blew the whistle to start the game. The first chance he got, Jeremy went for the puck, wove through the defencemen, passed the puck through their legs, spun around, skated forward, then backwards, then spun around again and . . . found himself in front of the net!

Nicholas was so surprised that he didn't have a chance to stop the puck. Jeremy shot and SCORED! His whole team cheered, even Dan.

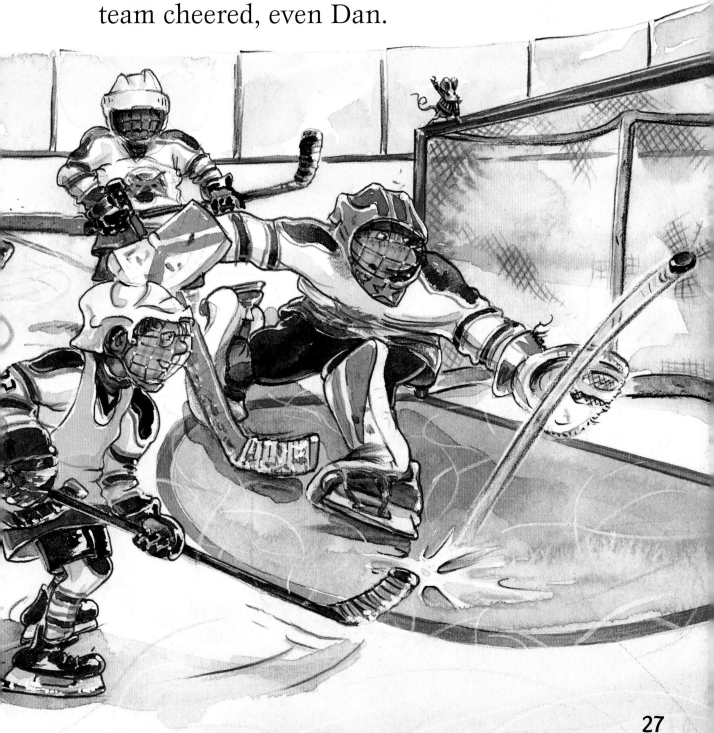

Jeremy scored two goals each period for a grand total of six goals! He was the highest scorer of the game!

At the final whistle, everyone rushed over and congratulated him. The celebration continued into the dressing room, where Big Dan lifted Jeremy up in the air. He was the hero of the day!

As for Nicholas . . .

. . . he had never been so happy to lose
a hockey game!